D1387795

Let There Be Reign

Johnny Hart and Brant Parker

CORONET BOOKS
Hodder Fawcett, London.

Copyright © 1972 Publishers Newspaper Syndicate
Copyright © 1977 CBS Publications, The Consumer
Publishing Division of CBS, Inc.

Published by special arrangement with
Field Newspaper Syndicate

First published 1977 by Fawcett Publications Inc.
New York

Coronet edition 1978
Third impression 1981

Printed and bound in Great Britain for
Hodder Fawcett Ltd,
Mill Road, Dunton Green, Sevenoaks,
Kent (Editorial Office: 47 Bedford
Square, London, WC1 3DP), by
Hunt Barnard Printing Ltd.,
Aylesbury, Bucks.

ISBN 0 340 23017 7

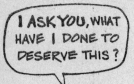

6-5

6-14

6-19

6-23

7-4

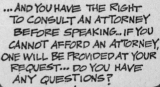

WHAT DO YOU THINK, DOC?

7·24

YOU MAY GO DOWN IN HISTORY, AS THE FIRST MAN TO COMMIT SUICIDE WITH BROWNIES.

HERBY WENT ON A 1200 CALORIE A DAY DIET...AND LOST **40** POUNDS.

HOW DOES HE FIGHT THE HUNGER PANGS?

EASY... AFTER THE SECOND SIX-PACK, HE PASSES OUT.

7-26

8-1

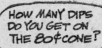

8-4

...IN THE BEGINNING, GOD CREATED HEAVEN AND EARTH...

...EXCEPT FOR THE MOON, WHICH WAS CREATED BY WALTER CRONKITE.

4

HOW CAN I BE SURE I AM GETTING 100% ORANGE JUICE?

8-18

BUY AN ORANGE.

8-24

9-11

A MESSAGE FROM OUR AMBASSADOR IN THE **CONGO**.

Dear King;
Relations with the natives is still shaky

they seem very restless.
Best to you,
Wiz, Duke,
ET AL

9-18

NOTIFY AL'S NEXT OF KIN.

9-19

9-20

9-21

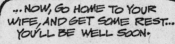

10·3

THE INSURANCE COMPANY NEEDS THREE ESTIMATES BEFORE I CAN GET THESE DENTS OUT OF MY ARMOUR

10-4

TELL 'EM $50..$60 AND $70

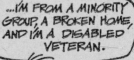

HOW'S THE WORLD TREATING YOU?

ROTTEN!

MAYBE IT'S JUST TRYING TO GET EVEN.

10-9

10-10

6

10-23

10·31

MIGRATING DOGS

7

WE CAUGHT THIS MAN VOTING TWICE!

FOR WHOM?

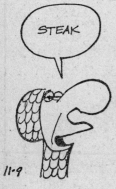

11-9

SIR... YOU'RE SUPPOSED TO LEAVE US 15%.

I'M SORRY, BUT I WAS HUNGRY.

11-14

11-17

11-21

THAT WILL BE $10.50

HOW COME THE SAME PRESCRIPTION IS ONLY $5.50 ACROSS THE STREET?

11·22

THEY GET MORE HYPOCHONDRIACS.

8

124

12-23

B.C RIGHT ON

JOHNNY HART

All these books are available at your local bookshop or newsagent, or can be ordered direct from the publisher. Just tick the titles you want and fill in the form below.

Prices and availability subject to change without notice.

CORONET BOOKS, P.O. Box 11, Falmouth, Cornwall.

Please send cheque or postal order, and allow the following for postage and packing:

U.K. – 40p for one book, plus 18p for the second book, and 13p for each additional book ordered up to a £1.49 maximum.

B.F.P.O. and EIRE – 40p for the first book, plus 18p for the second book, and 13p per copy for the next 7 books, 7p per book thereafter.

OTHER OVERSEAS CUSTOMERS – 60p for the first book, plus 18p per copy for each additional book.

Name ....

Address ....

....